The Sesame Street Pet Show

Featuring Jim Henson's Sesame Street Muppets

by Emily Perl Kingsley • Illustrated by Normand Chartier

LEMONADE

PET FOOD

WIN A PRIZE

BRING YOUR PET

A SESAME STREET/GOLDEN PRESS BOOK
Published by Western Publishing Company, Inc.
in conjunction with Children's Television Workshop.

It was the day of Sesame Street's big pet show. Ernie was on his way to the show, clutching a brown paper bag, when he saw Bert standing on the street corner.

"Come down here, Bernice. Come down!" called Bert to his pet pigeon. "I want to straighten out your beautiful feathers so you'll look your best."

Bernice landed on Bert's finger and cooed happily as he smoothed her feathers. "Look at her, Ernie," said Bert. "No pet at the show will be able to fly as high as Bernice can. She is sure to win the prize. Hey, Ernie, where is *your* pet?"

"He's right here, Bert, right inside this paper bag. But you can't see him until the show," said Ernie. "I want him to be a surprise. See you later, Bert."

Ernie walked down Sesame Street and passed Big Bird, who was talking into a fishbowl. "That's right, Goldie, another few laps," Big Bird said to his pet fish, who was swimming furiously back and forth in the bowl. "I bet no other pet at the show will be able to swim as fast as you can. You're sure to win the prize."

Ernie held up his bag. "My pet can't swim," said Ernie, "but he's going to win the prize anyway."

"Hey, Ernie," said Cookie Monster, who was standing next to a bird cage with a parrot in it. "Me have *talking* pet for pet show. Patricia the Parrot get prize at show!"

"Gee," said Ernie. "My pet can't talk, but he'll still win the prize."

Rodeo Rosie rode past on her horse. "Lance can gallop so fast," she called to Ernie, "that I know he's going to win the prize at the show."

"Rufus," Ernie said to the paper bag,
"I know you're not as fast as Lance,
but I still think you'll win."

Meanwhile, Oscar was leaning out of his can talking to his pet skunk.

"You really smell *yucchy*, Daisy," Oscar said. "You're gonna be the winner at the pet show!"

"Hi, Ernie," said Herry Monster. "Come look at my sweet little kitty. Sam can wash his face with his paw. I'm sure he's going to win the prize at the pet show."

"Gee, Herry, my pet can't wash his face. But I think he's going to win, anyway."

Then Ernie saw Grover and his pet. "Hi, Ernie,"
said Grover. "Look at my furry little puppy, Floyd.
He is sooo cute and adorable I just know he will
win the prize!"

Ernie sat down in the playground swing.
"Gee," he said to himself. "My pet can't coo,
can't swim, can't talk, can't gallop, can't wash his
face, and he isn't even furry...."

The Count was busy getting his pet ready for the pet show. "Hold still, Octavia. I want to tie a ribbon on each of your lovely arms! There...that's one arm...two arms...three...stop wiggling, Octavia darling! Four, five, six, seven, *eight!* Eight beautiful arms! Surely you will win the prize."

When Ernie saw Betty Lou, she was coaching her pet frog.

"Come on, Louise. You can hop higher than that!" she said. "Oh, hi, Ernie. Look what Louise can do. I bet she'll win the prize at the pet show."

At last Ernie arrived at the show.

"Line up, everybody," said Sherlock Hemlock, who was the judge. "Is everybody ready? The Sesame Street pet show is about to begin!"

Judge Sherlock Hemlock began to move slowly down the line, looking carefully at every pet.

"Egad!" said Sherlock, as he watched Goldie swim a lap.

"Eight arms? Incredible!" he remarked as he examined Octavia the octopus.

"Cute and furry indeed!" he said, inspecting Grover's puppy, Floyd.

"Ah-hum! I have made up my mind!" announced Sherlock when he reached the end of the line.

The Sesame Street Pet Show

"The prize for the HIGHEST FLYER goes to Bert's pigeon, Bernice!

"The prize for the BEST SWIMMER is won by Big Bird's goldfish, Goldie.

"Cookie Monster's parrot, Patricia, wins the prize for BEST TALKER and Rodeo Rosie's horse, Lance, wins the prize for FASTEST!

"Daisy, Oscar's skunk, wins SMELLIEST and Sam, Herry's kitten, wins CLEANEST.

"Grover's puppy, Floyd, is definitely the FURRIEST pet. Octavia the Octopus, the Count's pet, wins the prize for MOST ARMS, and Betty Lou's frog, Louise, wins the BEST HOPPER prize.

"Everyone's pet is special," said Sherlock Hemlock, giving blue ribbons to all the pets. "Everyone's pet wins a prize!"

"Wait!" cried Ernie. "You haven't seen *my* pet yet!"

Ernie took a glass jar out of his brown paper bag. The top of the jar had holes punched in it. He unscrewed the top and dumped out a small brown bug.

"This is Rufus," said Ernie.

"That's your pet?" asked Betty Lou. "A little brown bug?"

"Don't tell me that boring bug is your terrific pet!" said Oscar.

"What kind of prize can your bug win, Ernie?" asked Big Bird.

Then Rufus began to glow.
"Oh, my goodness!" shouted
Grover. "He lights up!"
"To Rufus the firefly," said
Sherlock Hemlock, "I award the
prize of BRIGHTEST PET!"
"Hooray!" shouted everyone.

BRIGHTEST
PET